W9-APO-820

Angelina and the Butterfly

Story adapted by KATHARINE HOLABIRD from the TV episode
written by Sally-Ann Lever

BASED ON THE CLASSIC PICTURE BOOKS
BY KATHARINE HOLABIRD AND HELEN CRAIG

PLEASANT COMPANY PUBLICATIONS™

Published by Pleasant Company Publications
First published in Great Britain by Penguin Books Ltd., 2002
© 2002 HIT Entertainment PLC
Based on the illustrations by Helen Craig and the text by Katharine Holabird

Angelina, Angelina Ballerina, and the Dancing Angelina logo are trademarks of HIT Entertainment PLC,
Katharine Holabird, and Helen Craig. Angelina is registered in the U.K. and Japan and with the USPTO.
The Dancing Angelina logo is registered in the U.K.

Visit our Web site at **www.americangirl.com**
and Angelina's very own site at **www.angelinaballerina.com**

Manufactured in Hong Kong.
02 03 04 05 06 07 08 09 C&C 10 9 8 7 6 5 4 3 2 1

First Pleasant Company printing, 2002

Library of Congress Cataloging-in-Publication Data
Holabird, Katharine
Angelina and the butterfly / story adapted by Katharine Holabird from the CiTV episode written by Sally-Ann Lever.
p. cm.
"Based on the classic picture books by Katharine Holabird and Helen Craig."
"An Angelina ballerina storybook."
Summary: When Angelina the mouse finds a pink butterfly with a twisted leg, she's determined to look after it
and keep it forever until a surprising turn of events sets the butterfly free.
ISBN 1-58485-618-1
[1. Mice—Fiction. 2. Butterflies—Fiction.] I. Lever, Sally-Ann. II. Craig, Helen, ill. III. Title.

PZ7.H689 Alg 2002
[E]—dc21   2001059809

"What a perfect day!" Angelina smiled at her best friend, Alice. Angelina always loved to go on Miss Lilly's special picnics in Big Wood with her friends from ballet school, and today even her little cousin, Henry, was invited to join in the fun.

The hungry mouselings very quickly ate all the delicious pies and cakes. Then Angelina and her friends jumped up to play.

"Oh, look!" cried Angelina, as a large pink butterfly landed on her paw. "Isn't he beautiful?"

Everyone crowded around to admire the lovely butterfly.

"Can I hold him, Angelina?" begged Henry.

"Absolutely not!" said Angelina. "Look! He's damaged his leg. You might hurt him." She showed her friends the butterfly's twisted leg.

"I'm going to have to look after him myself," Angelina declared. And she carried the hurt butterfly very carefully all the way back to her cottage, with Henry and Alice following behind.

"I'm calling my butterfly Arthur," Angelina told her parents. "King of all the flowers, trees, and sky."

Mr. Mouseling found Arthur a large glass jar, and Mrs. Mouseling brought Arthur some leaves.

"Please can I put Arthur in the jar?" Henry asked, jumping up and down with excitement.

Angelina shook her head. "You might drop him," she said as she gently put Arthur in the jar herself. "And now he needs to stay in his house and rest," Angelina added firmly.

The next morning when they looked in the jar, Arthur was beating his wings against the glass.

"Arthur's flying!" cried Henry happily.

"Maybe he wants to go back to his family," said Alice.

But Angelina knew better. "This is his home now," she reminded them.

Angelina and Alice went to have their breakfast, while Henry sneaked back into the room to have another peek at Arthur. Very carefully, he lifted the lid off the jar for a better look. PING!

The lid sailed into the air, and Arthur flew out of the jar.

"Oh no!" cried Henry. "Come back, Arthur!"

Henry chased the butterfly around and around Angelina's room, but Arthur was too fast for him.

Then, just as Angelina came through the door to see what all the noise was about, Arthur flew out the window and disappeared.

"HENRY!" cried Angelina.

"I'm sorry!" wailed Henry. "It was an accident."

"We have to find Arthur!" Angelina shouted, and she raced out the door with Henry just behind her.

The two mouselings ran up and down the cobbled streets of Chipping Cheddar, looking everywhere and asking everyone, but no one had seen a pink butterfly. Angelina was so tired, she sat down and burst into tears. "Arthur's gone forever," she sobbed.

enry tried to think of something nice to say. "Maybe Arthur's gone back to Big Wood," he whispered.

Angelina jumped to her feet. "That's it!" she cried, and she raced off down the road again, with Henry running as fast as he could to catch up.

They reached the woods just as it was getting dark. Angelina thought she saw something pink in the bushes and ran to catch it. "ARTHUUURRR!" she shouted. But Angelina's feet got tangled in the creepers. Then she tripped over a log and fell head over heels into a deep, dark pit.

Henry rushed after her and bravely reached down to save her when . . . OOPS! He tumbled into the pit himself and landed with a thump next to Angelina.

"Ouch!" he cried.

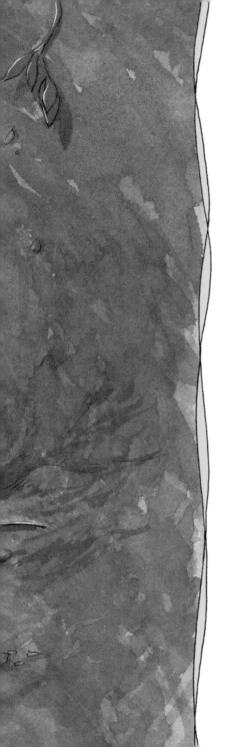

It was cold and muddy down in the pit, and much too deep for them to climb out.

"I'm scared!" Henry whimpered.

Suddenly Angelina wasn't angry with Henry anymore, and she gave him a cuddle. "Don't worry, Henry," said Angelina, even though she felt worried, too.

"I'm really sorry about losing Arthur," Henry sniffed in a tiny voice.

"It's okay, Henry," Angelina forgave him. "I know you didn't mean to lose him."

As the hours ticked by, everyone in the village came to join the search for the two lost mouselings.

"They're not at my house," panted Alice.

"And they're not down by Miller's Pond," sighed William.

"Oh, where could they be?" cried Miss Lilly, wiping away her tears.

Suddenly Alice looked up, and there was Arthur fluttering just over her head.

"Quick!" she shouted. "Let's follow Arthur!"

The butterfly flew off toward the woods, and everyone scrambled through the mud behind him. Before long, they could hear Angelina and Henry's shouts for help.

"Thank goodness you're alive!" cried Miss Lilly as Mr. Mouseling pulled the two mouselings out of the pit.

"But how did you find us?" asked Angelina.

"Arthur showed us the way," smiled Alice.

Everyone looked up to thank the butterfly, but Arthur was already gone. Poor Angelina burst into tears.

The next day when Henry and Alice came over, Angelina was still thinking about her butterfly.

"I don't suppose I'll ever see Arthur again," she sighed. Just then, a beautiful pink butterfly appeared and perched on the tip of her nose.

"It's Arthur!" cried Henry. "Let's put him back in the jar!"

"No!" cried out Angelina.

"But he'll fly away again," Henry whimpered.

"I know," said Angelina, "but being trapped is awful, and to be happy, butterflies need to be free."

Then Angelina waved good-bye, and Arthur fluttered back up to the sky and joined a crowd of beautifully colored dancing butterflies.